Lincoln Township Library
2099 W. John Beers Rd.
Stevensville, MI 49127

W9-BAI-731

Copy 2

E
636.8
SEL
    Selsam, Millicent E.
      How kittens grow / by Millicent E. Selsam ;
    photographs by Neil Johnson. -- New York :
    Scholastic, 1992.
      unp : col. ill. ; 21 cm.

      c2 Midwest 6-17-94 $13.49.
      ISBN 0-590-44784-X.

225

      1.Cats.  I.Title.

0694 sja

# How Kittens Grow

By Millicent E. Selsam
Photographs by Neil Johnson

Lincoln Township Library
2099 W. John Beers Rd.
Stevensville, MI 49127
429-9575

**SCHOLASTIC INC.**

New York Toronto London Auckland Sydney

*The author wishes to thank Dr. Jay S. Rosenblatt,
Professor of Psychology, Institute of Animal
Behavior, Rutgers State University, for reading
the manuscript of this book.*

No part of this publication may be reproduced in whole or in
part, or stored in a retrieval system, or transmitted in any
form or by any means, electronic, mechanical, photocopying,
recording, or otherwise, without written permission of the
publisher. For information regarding permission, write to
Scholastic, Inc., 730 Broadway, New York, NY 10003.

ISBN 0-590-44784-X

Text copyright © 1973 by Millicent E. Selsam.
Photographs copyright © 1992 by Neil Johnson.
All rights reserved. Published by Scholastic Inc.
CARTWHEEL BOOKS is a trademark of Scholastic Inc.

12 11 10 9 8 7 6 5 4 3 2      2 3 4 5 6/9

Printed in the U.S.A.      24

First Scholastic printing, November 1992

# How Kittens Grow

Mother cat has just given
birth to these four kittens.
She lies on her side and
licks them off.

Each kitten is tiny.
It cannot see because its eyes are closed.
It cannot hear because its ears are closed.
But the kitten can smell, and touch, and feel warmth.

Each kitten crawls toward Mother's warm body.
Its front legs move forward slowly.
It drags its hind legs along.
Its head moves from side to side.
At last it reaches Mother cat.

Now the kittens nuzzle in Mother cat's fur with
their noses and mouths.
They keep nuzzling until they touch a nipple.
Then they grab the nipple with their mouths
and begin to suck milk.
Each kitten sucks milk within an hour after it is born.

These tiny kittens need their mother.
She nurses them.
She keeps them warm.
She keeps them safe.

For four days Mother cat stays with
the kittens almost all the time.
About every two hours she gets up.
She stretches.
Then she goes off to eat something.

After the fourth day, she gets up more often.
The kittens sleep while she is away.
They usually sleep on top of one another.
They keep warm that way.

When Mother cat
comes back,
she licks the kittens.
This wakes them up.
Then Mother cat
lies down
and the kittens
suck milk again.

By this time
each kitten
has learned to nurse
at its own
special nipple.
If another kitten
tries to take its place,
it holds on tight
and will not let go.

When the kittens are about two weeks old,
their eyes have opened.
Their ears are open, too.

The kittens are growing.
They weigh twice as much now
as they weighed when they were born.

The kittens still crawl.
They cannot walk yet.
But they are beginning
to see more and hear more.

Sometimes a kitten crawls
away from Mother.
But then the floor feels cold.
And the floor smells different.
The kitten cries.
Mother cat hears it.
She goes to it and carries it home
by the neck.

Now the kittens are
four weeks old.
They can go over to
Mother cat to nurse when
she does not come to them.
Each week they gain about
six ounces.

The kittens stand
on their feet and
walk slowly.
They are still wobbly.
But they see pretty well.
And they hear very well.

Mother cat goes to the kittens less and less.
But the kittens can follow her around now,
and make her lie down and let them nurse.
They still nurse at their own special nipples.

Now the kittens can play
with each other.
They lick each other.
They chase each other.
They roll over each other.

They play with everything they can find.

They run after Mother cat.
They jump on her.
They lick her face.
They bite her tail.

Sometimes the playing
gets too rough.
Then Mother cat jumps
away from the kittens.
She jumps on a high stool,
or up to a shelf.
Sometimes she swats
the kittens.

When the kittens are five weeks old,
they are getting less milk from their mother.
But they can drink milk from a saucer.

They follow Mother cat
when she goes to feed.
Sometimes they step
in the food dish.
Sometimes they step on
some food on the floor.
Then they lick their paws.
The food tastes good!
Sometimes they lick
Mother's mouth and
taste the food that way.
That is how they learn
to eat solid food.

On farms, cats hunt their own food.
At first, Mother cat brings live animals back to the kittens.
They learn to know the food they will later hunt themselves.
Then the kittens begin to follow Mother
when she goes to find food.

That is how they learn
to hunt and kill small
animals, especially mice.
The kittens have teeth
now and can chew.
These are baby teeth
at first, just as yours are.
When a cat is about
six months old,
the baby teeth fall out
and the adult teeth
take their place.

When the kittens are about eight weeks old,
they have stopped getting milk from their mother.
They have learned to eat solid food.
They can chase, climb, leap, run, move quietly
through the grass, and pounce on a mouse.

They can do everything a grown-up cat can do.
This is the best time to get a kitten.

Lincoln Township Library
2099 W. John Beers Rd.
Stevensville, MI 49127
429-9575